BITTEN BY THE DOCTOR

ASPEN RIDGE PACK: SHIFTER MD
BOOK 1

LUNA WILDER

Copyright © 2021 by Luna Wilder

www.lunawilderbooks.com

All Rights Reserved. No part of this book may be reproduced in any form or by any electronic or mechanical means, including information storage and retrieval systems, without written permission from the author, except for the use of brief quotations in a book review. Please do not participate in or encourage piracy of copyrighted materials in violation of the author's rights. All characters and storylines are the property of the author and your support and respect are appreciated. The characters and events portrayed in this book are fictitious. Any similarity to real persons, living or dead, is coincidental and not intended by the author.

*

Can he take away her choice, even if it means saving her life?

Being a doctor and finding his mate is all that Roman Michaels has ever wanted.

He's accomplished the first but is still searching for the second.

Then there's an avalanche in Aspen Ridge, the tiny town where his pack is located, and Iggy Jones is wheeled in.

As soon as he sees her, he knows she's the one for him.

There's just one problem.

She's a human and unconscious.

Biting her will save her life, but it will also force her to be his mate, something he's sure she knows nothing about.

Can he really take away her choice? Does he have any other option?

ONE

Iggy

"ARE you sure that you have everything packed?" My mom asks distractedly.

She's staring at another late notice from our landlord, and my stomach clenches with guilt when I see the stressed, slightly panicked look in her eyes. It's one that I recognize well by now, but it still leaves an aching hole in my stomach each time.

Maybe I shouldn't be taking this trip. I can give them the money and we can try to get caught up on some of these bills.

I'm the reason that we're in this mess in the first place. I was born with a hole in my heart, and my parents went bankrupt trying to keep me alive. It was fixed, but I've spent the rest of my life trying to make up for putting them in this situation.

"I'm sure," I say, swallowing around the lump in my throat.

It may be selfish, but I've been scrimping and saving for

months to go see my best friend, Rue, and I'm not missing this opportunity. I know that my mom wouldn't take my money anyway. She's the one who has been pushing me to go out and live my own life. This trip is my one small taste of being away from my parents and all the problems here at home.

"Drive safe. And be sure to call me as soon as you get there."

"I will," I promise her, and she wraps her thin arms around me, squeezing me tight.

I breathe in her familiar rose scent before I pull away.

"I'll see you in a few days!" I promise her, and she nods, tucking the bills behind her back as she waves goodbye.

Anchorage is only a few hours from Aspen Ridge, and I pull up by GPS, typing in Rue's new address before I back out of the driveway and hit the road.

Rue and I have been best friends forever, and I was both happy and jealous when she left and moved away from our hometown. I know that she needed to. Her dad would have killed her or forced her to move out sooner or later, and I'm glad she's safe now. I just wish that I also got to leave and have my own adventure. This trip is my chance to do that before I have to head back to Anchorage and my boring job.

I sing along with the radio as I drive through snow-covered roads and highways. The sun is starting to shine from behind the clouds as I pull up in front of Rue's new place. Well, actually, it's her boyfriends' new place. I can't wait to meet them. She's been uncharacteristically vague about them, and I miss the days when we used to share everything.

The house is a nice two-story cabin nestled in the woods. I almost drove past it, and there doesn't seem to be much of anything else on this road so I'm glad I didn't. The houses out here are spaced far apart, and I look around as I climb out of my little hatchback.

"Iggy!" Rue yells as she comes running out of the house.

I turn, laughing, when I see her red hair blowing around her face. Her blue eyes sparkle as she practically launches herself at me, and I grin, wrapping my arms around her.

"I missed you," I say, and my throat threatens to close up.

I've been keeping things light, but I know how bad things are back home. I wish she was still there so we could sneak out and talk about our problems but I guess that's changed now too.

"I missed you too! I'm so happy that you're here."

"We'll get the bags," a guy says, and I turn, my jaw dropping when I see the two huge men standing there.

"Thanks. Iggy, this is Bo and Liam," Rue says, nodding to both of them. "Guys, this is my best friend, Iggy."

"It's nice to finally meet you," Bo says with a friendly smile, and I relax instantly.

"Rue has told us a lot about you. I hope you didn't have any trouble finding the place," Liam says as he grabs my small suitcase.

"No, the GPS led me right here," I say as we head up the front porch steps and inside.

"I'll show you around," Rue says as she grabs my hand and tugs me up the stairs. "You'll be staying in here."

I look around the guest room, and my eyes almost bug out of my head. This room is at least twice the size of my room back home, and envy slithers through me like a snake.

"It's awesome," I tell Rue, and she smiles.

"Are you hungry or anything? We could grab something to eat, and then I can show you around town."

"Sure. I wanted to try skiing while I was here."

"We can go today," Rue promises as I follow her back downstairs.

"Where are we going?" Liam asks.

"Skiing."

He frowns, but Rue ignores him and leads me into the kitchen.

"What are you hungry for?" She asks.

"Maybe just a sandwich?"

"Sure thing."

I look around the kitchen while she makes us sandwiches. Bo and Liam are hovering around her, and I wonder if they think I'm going to try to tempt her back to Anchorage. No matter how much I miss her, I could never do that. She's blossomed since she's been here. I've never heard or seen her so happy.

Light snowflakes are starting to come down outside, or maybe they're just blowing off the trees. Either way, it makes me feel like I'm in a snow globe, and I smile.

I wish I could live somewhere like this.

Our house is practically a closet compared to this place, and that familiar pang of resentment and guilt hits me. I've been dealing with these feelings my whole life. I can still remember the first time I went over to someone's house for a birthday party and realized that my family was different.

"Food's done," Rue says, and I push my thoughts aside as I paste a smile on my face and turn around.

"Thanks. How are you liking Aspen Ridge?" I ask her as we sit down at the kitchen table.

"It's not where I thought I would settle down, but I love it. Everyone is really friendly."

"And it's close enough for me to come visit," I add, and she laughs.

"Exactly."

We finish off our sandwiches, and both head upstairs to bundle up.

"We'll come with you," Bo and Liam say, and I look away as they both wrap their arms around Rue and head into their bedroom. It feels so intimate to watch. I was their biggest fan when Rue told me she was thinking about being with two men. I still think she's awesome for bucking tradition and following her heart.

It's obvious that Bo and Liam worship her, and Rue is practically glowing. I wish I could have that too. I haven't been on a date in, well, forever. There hasn't been time. I've been working since I was fifteen, trying to help support my family.

It's not like I had many options anyway. Rue and I were the outcasts at our school. We never had money to do anything like field trips or go out to the movies. We were always in thrift store clothes or hand-me-downs.

I was lucky that I had Rue. At least then I wasn't alone.

I head into the guest room and unzip my suitcase. I brought my snow gear since I wasn't sure what we would be doing, but I was sure that there would be snow. It's still snowing almost every day in Alaska.

I can hear Rue and the guys moving around outside the door, and I hurry to pull on my boots and hat. I braid my blonde hair so that it's out of my face before I head to meet them.

"All set?" Liam asks as I come downstairs, and I smile.

"Yep, how far to the slopes?" I ask as I follow them out to their Jeep.

"About twenty minutes. It's on the other side of town," Bo says as he opens the back door for me and Rue.

We settle in, and I catch Rue up on life back in Anchorage as we head to the ski resort.

"Dad has been picking up more shifts so I haven't seen him a ton lately. My mom says hi, by the way."

"Aw, tell her that I said hi too!"

"I will," I promise.

"What are Alex and Sarah up to?" She asks as we drive down Main Street.

Sarah and Alex are my older brother and sister. We're not as close as I'd like us to be, and I know that it's because everything changed when I came along. I can't really blame them. I took up more of my parent's time and attention when I was sick. I took up more money and space. Still, it's hard to see their close relationship and know we'll never have that.

"They're still working at the Old Mill and Bar downtown. Sarah has been seeing that James Young guy. I don't know if you remember him?"

"Yeah, he was in the year above us, right?" She asks, and I nod.

"Yeah, he seems nice enough. I've only met him once, but he seems to treat her well."

She nods as Liam pulls into a parking spot up front, and we all hop out.

"We'll pay. You guys want to go pick out your ski stuff?" Bo asks, and Rue nods, taking my hand and dragging me over to the rows of skis and poles.

"Have you been here before?" I ask, and she shakes her head.

"No, it was storming when I first got here, and then, well, we've been a little busy," she says, her cheeks flaming, and I grin.

"You go, girl!" I cheer, and she laughs.

"It's been an...adjustment," she says, but she's smiling, and I know she's been enjoying her time here.

"Brag."

Rue giggles at that, and I grab a pair of skis and some poles.

"Are these right?" I ask Rue, and she shrugs, looking just as confused by all of this as I am.

Neither of us has ever been skiing, but it's been on my bucket list, and when I found out that Aspen Ridge actually had a really nice ski resort, I was excited to give it a try. I've been saving up for weeks to be able to afford it, and I'm grateful that Bo and Liam are covering it. Now I'll be able to have some money to give my parents when I get home.

"Ready to go?" Bo asks as he comes over with two wristbands for us.

I put mine on and follow behind everyone as we head over to the ski lift. Nerves start to hit me as I watch the people in front of us easily hop on.

"Are you as nervous as I am about this?" Rue asks, and I giggle.

"More. Do you think that we'll look that graceful when we do it?" I whisper back, and she laughs.

"Probably more graceful, actually. Like models."

I chuckle. Neither Rue nor I would ever be mistaken for models. We're about ten sizes too big for that. We've always been curvy. I'm not sure if it was stress eating our way through high school or just that we could only really afford crap food.

"We'll show you two how it's done," Bo says as they ski over to the lift and wait for the seat to come.

I've actually been doing pretty good on skiing, though we've been on flat land this whole time. We're headed up to the bunny hill, and Bo and Liam are going to show us how to tackle one of these hills.

"Ready for this?" Rue asks as the boys' lift starts to rise into the air.

"I think so?"

"If you fall on your ass, I'll do the same," she promises, and I grin.

"That's why we're best friends."

We get into position, and my heart is racing as we wait for the lift to come by. It does, and I squeak as I land on the hard, cold seat, and Rue is clinging to the side like she's afraid she's going to fall out at any second.

"We did it!" I whisper yell at her as we rise into the sky.

She smiles, but there's something tense in the way she's looking at me.

"I uh, I need to talk to you about something, but, uh, I'm starting to think that I don't like heights," Rue whispers back, and she looks pretty pale.

"We can talk once we're on solid ground. We're almost there," I say, reaching over and grabbing her hand.

She squeezes my hand, and I let her try to break my fingers as we head toward the first stop.

"Oh crap. We have to hop off," I say, and she stares at me with wide eyes.

"What happens if we don't?"

"Uh, I think we just keep going around in circles until we die."

"Well, that kind of happens regardless," she quips, and I laugh.

"Okay, we can do this. One," I start.

"Two," she says, and together we jump on three.

Neither of us would land on our skis if Bo and Liam weren't there to catch us and keep us upright.

"Thanks," I tell Bo, and he smiles.

"Of course. You're doing great."

His words make me feel better, and we slowly make our way over to the edge of the hill.

"So, you want to take it easy the first few times. You can use your poles to push off," Liam says as he walks us through how to speed up and slow down.

"Now I want pizza," Rue whispers to me once he's done, and I laugh.

"I've already forgotten if it's the little pizza slice to speed up or slow down," I whisper back, and she giggles.

"I'll go first," Bo says, and we watch as he easily skis down to the bottom of the little hill.

"Ready to try?" Liam asks Rue, and she takes a deep breath but nods.

"Alright, let's do this," Rue says, and I cheer for her as she and Liam start to make their way slowly down the hill.

"Woohoo!" I shout once they make it down to the bottom.

"It wasn't so bad! You can do it!" She yells back, and I take a deep breath, trying to shake off the nerves as I grip my poles and inch my way toward the hill.

A cracking sound starts, and I turn around, trying to figure out where it came from, when a gust of white hits me, knocking me back on my skis. The last thing I remember before everything went dark was seeing the sky turn white as snow covered me.

TWO

Roman

"ARE YOU HEADED OUT TOO?" Jax asks as he slides his jacket on.

"No, I just got here a few hours ago. I have another four before I'm off," I tell him, and he claps me on my shoulder.

Jax and I have been close friends for the last few years. We started at the Aspen Ridge Hospital around the same time, and we clicked right away. Since we both spend most of our time here, he's become one of my closest friends.

"It was pretty slow during my shift," he says, and I glare at him.

"Sure, rub it in," I grumble, and he smirks at me.

"Maybe it will be slow for you too."

"There was an avalanche on Hunter Mountain," the head nurse announces, and Jax and I both snap to attention. "Ambulances are inbound!"

I look at Jax, and he grumbles about how he should have

left earlier as he heads back to the changing room to get his things back on.

I jog down the hallway to the ambulance bay along with the other doctors on staff.

"I heard the roads are getting bad. They can't call in anyone else to help," I overhear Asher tell Micah, and I groan.

That means that things are going to be crazy around here.

"Have we heard how many casualties there were?" I ask them, and they shrug.

"I just heard that it was by the ski resort," Micah says, and I nod as the doors open and the first patient is rolled in on the gurney.

As soon as her scent hits me, my wolf snaps inside of me and I jump forward.

"Mine!" I yell, grabbing the stretcher and pulling it into the first hospital room.

My brain is spinning, and I grit my teeth, holding my wolf back as I stare down at my mate. Seeing her curves has my mouth watering, and I want to slap myself. Now is not the time to be checking her out.

Her blonde hair is twisted and matted to the side of her head, covering her face. There's blood on her forehead, and I force my wolf to stand down.

Let's get her bandaged up, then we can focus on claiming her, I tell him, and he growls but relents. He paces back and forth inside of me, and I try to ignore him as best as I can as I tend to my pretty mate.

The cut on her head is deep, and I disinfect my hands, putting on gloves as I tell the nurse to hand me some wipes and the stapler. The nurse passes me a needle, and I brush her hair away from her face so that I can insert the needle and numb the area.

I disinfect and staple the gash and start to assess her other injuries.

"She was out in the snow for a while," the nurse tells me, and I want to wrap my body around hers to warm her up.

"Get more blankets. Do we have any information on her?" I ask, trying to stay all business so I don't get distracted by trying to bite her when I should be saving her life.

Though biting her would save her life. It would pass on some of my shifter qualities, like advanced healing.

We can't bite her, though, I tell my wolf, and he snarls. *She's obviously a human, and she's probably a tourist here for the ski resort. She has no clue about shifters, and we can't freak her out. Not if we want a chance with her.*

We've always wanted to find our fated mate, and we've been searching for years, but we hadn't been able to find her. I had actually just promised myself this morning that I would take a vacation soon so I could try to go out and find her. Now she's fallen into our lap, and it's bittersweet.

Part of the problem is that we're so busy as a doctor, but now that she's here, I'm already working on how to rework my schedule to spend more time with her.

Her scent hits my nose, and this time it's different. She's dying. Panic floods me, and I hurry to find out what's wrong. I listen to her heart, lungs, and stomach, and that's when I see she's bleeding from her back.

"Help me get her onto her side," I demand, and the nurses hurry to help me roll her over.

"Shit," Jax says when he comes in and sees the branch sticking out of her back.

"She's mine," I snap at him, and he blinks.

It takes him a second to understand what I mean, and I can see what it dawns on him in his eyes.

"Got it," he says as he hurries to help me save her life.

"We need to pull it out."

He nods, pulling on his own gloves as we survey the wound. The next two hours pass in a blur as we remove the branch and try to stop the bleeding.

"She's lost a lot of blood," Jax whispers, and I grit my teeth.

My wolf has gone from pacing and snarling at me to watching in agony.

"You need to bite her," Jax whispers, and I shake my head.

"She's a human," I whisper back as he clamps another cut on her kidney.

"She's also half frozen and bleeding internally," he snaps at me, and I know he's right. "It's the only way to save her."

Indecision weighs on me as I study her pale face. The heart monitor is beeping slower and slower, and I know she's getting weaker.

If I want to save her life, I need to bite her, but if I do that, will she ever be able to forgive me? What happens if she decides to leave after she's better? I would never be able to survive that.

"Roman!" Jax snaps as the monitors start to go crazy.

"Fuck," I yell as I move closer to her.

All of the nurses here are shifters too, and I know they won't freak out if I bite her. My wolf leaps to his feet inside me as I bend over, my teeth elongating as I get ready to bite her.

I never thought I would have to force the mating bond

with my mate, but I don't have a choice here. Not if I want to *have* a mate.

With a deep breath and a sinking feeling in my gut, I sink my teeth into her neck.

THREE

Iggy

I GROAN as my eyelids flutter open, and I stare up at the generic white ceiling. It takes me a second to realize where I am, but the beeping heart monitor kind of gives it away. I've heard that sound a lot in my short life.

I try to sit up and wince, sinking back against the bed. Everything is sore, and I search my brain, trying to remember what happened. How did I end up here?

"Easy," comes a deep voice to my left, and I turn to take in the stranger.

"Who are you?" I ask, my voice coming out rusty.

"I'm Roman. Dr. Roman," he amends, and he seems almost nervous for some reason.

Seeing him like that only endears me to him, and I nod. He shifts on his feet, and I take the time to study him.

He's hot. Like really hot.

Dark brown hair is hanging across his forehead, and he watches me with tired green eyes. He looks like he hasn't slept all night, and I start to get worried. Maybe my injuries are worse than I thought.

"Am I dying?" I blurt out, and he looks alarmed.

"What? No! No, you're going to be fine."

"Oh."

I look away, my heart starting to slide back down to my chest from where it was lodged in my throat, and I take a deep breath.

My eyes are drawn back to Roman, and I can't seem to look away from him. I've seen a lot of hot guys in my life, but I've never once felt a pull to one like this. It's like we're two magnets being drawn together.

I wonder how crazy I would sound if I asked him if he felt that way too.

Probably pretty crazy! Play it cool! I warn myself, and I clear my throat.

"What happened?" I ask instead.

"There was an avalanche. You got swept along with it and had some internal injuries," he says, and I get the feeling that he's downplaying how bad it was.

"Iggy!" Rue says as she comes barreling into the room. "Thank god you're alright!"

"Are you okay?" I ask her, and she nods.

"Yeah, just a few scratches, but then we couldn't get across town to the hospital. I've been so worried," she says, and the door opens again.

Bo and Liam walk in, their faces looking relieved when they see I'm awake and okay.

"Do you need anything?" Liam asks me, and Roman growls at him.

Like legit growls.

My core clenches, and I stare at him in shock.

"Am I not allowed to eat or drink anything?" I ask him, and he blinks.

"I'll get you something."

He stalks out of the room, and I frown as I watch him go. I wonder what's up with him. He went from being sweet and almost doting to kind of grumpy and distant.

"Do you know him?" I ask Bo and Liam.

Maybe he doesn't like them for some reason. Bo and Liam seem really nice, though, so I don't know why Roman would have an issue with them.

"No, not really," Bo says as he drags a chair over for Rue to sit in.

The air conditioning kicks on, and I shiver.

"We'll go get you a blanket," Liam says, and Bo follows him out of the room.

"They were really worried about you, too," Rue says, and I smile.

"I'm okay. Really."

"Visiting hours are almost over, but I'm hoping they'll let us stay. It took us forever to get through all the traffic and snow."

"That bad?"

"Yeah, there's been a few bad storms and avalanches before this, but this one was by far the worst."

"I don't remember any of it," I admit, and she nods, reaching over to take my hand in hers.

"That might be for the best. It all happened so fast that I barely saw what had happened. You were there one second and gone the next," she says, and her eyes fill with tears.

"I hope that everyone else is alright," I whisper, and she nods.

"They were all brought here, I think. It's the only hospital in the area."

"I'm surprised that Dr. Roman was in here then. I'd think he would be too busy to sit with one of his patients."

Rue shrugs, but she has this look in her eye that says that she might know something that I don't.

"What did you want to talk about?" I ask, remembering how nervous she had seemed on the ski lift.

"Oh, I—"

"Got the blanket and some other stuff," Bo says in an upbeat voice as he comes into the room.

He sets the flowers down on the bedside table, and I smile. No one has ever given me flowers before, and I reach out to feel the petals.

"Thanks. They're beautiful," I say, and he grins.

"I got you a bear," Liam says, and he passes me the teddy bear holding a heart that says get well soon.

"Aww, thank you!"

"We also got you a sweater and this throw blanket," he says, passing Rue the blanket.

She tucks me in, and I laugh as I run my fingers over the soft fabric.

"Thanks, guys. You didn't have to do all of this."

"We're just glad that you're okay," Bo says.

The door opens again, and my heart kicks against my ribs as I turn to see if it's Roman coming back. It's not, and I try not to frown as a nurse bustles in.

"How are you feeling, dear?" She asks me, and I smile.

"I'm fine. Do you think that I'll be ready to leave soon?" I ask, and she shakes her head.

"We'll have to wait for Dr. Michaels to answer that, but I imagine it would be at least overnight."

I nod as she marks something down on my chart.

"Visiting hours are over, so I'm afraid your guests will have to leave," she says apologetically, and I nod.

"We'll be back first thing tomorrow," Rue promises, and I nod.

"I'll see you then."

They all wave, and I try to get comfortable in the hospital bed once I'm alone. I burrow further under the throw blanket, and my eyes start to droop when the door opens, and Roman comes back in.

His eyes go right to the bouquet of flowers, and he frowns.

"Who are those from?"

"Bo," I say, twisting my new teddy bear between my fingers. "Aren't they pretty? No one has ever given me flowers before."

Roman tenses at my words, his frown intensifying, and I can swear that his eyes are almost glowing.

"And the teddy bear?" He grits out.

"Liam got that for me. Wasn't that sweet of him?"

He grunts an answer, and I frown. I see that he's still being grumpy.

"They really dote on Rue. It must be hard to turn off," I say, and he frowns.

"Who is Rue?"

"My best friend. Their girlfriend."

"Oh," he says, and he smiles as he grabs the tray and drags it over to the bed.

His mood swings are starting to throw me, and I try to catch up as he sets some food and a cup of water on the tray for me.

"Visiting hours are over," I tell him, and he nods.

"I know."

"Do you have other patients?"

"Yeah."

"Are you also delivering food to them?" I ask him, and

he stares at me like I'm the crazy one here.

"No, the nurses do that."

"Right," I say, staring down at the feast that he's laid out for me.

"You can eat. Just take it slow."

I nod, grabbing the spoon and the jello.

"I had you pinned as a pudding girl," he says, and I shrug.

"That's for dessert."

He nods, taking a seat in the chair that Rue just vacated, and I try to ignore the way he's staring at me as I finish off the jello cup.

"Are you staying in Aspen Ridge?" He asks, and I nod.

"Yeah, Rue just moved here, and I came to visit her."

"Where are you from originally?"

"Anchorage."

"Are you going to move out here too?" He asks, and I can swear he almost sounds hopeful.

"No, not right now, anyway."

"Why not?" He demands, and I stare at him.

"Um, why would I?" I counter, and he glares at the far wall.

What the hell is going on here?

"Have you lived here long?" I ask, trying to ease the tension in the room.

"Born and raised. I left for college and medical school, but this will always be home."

"That's nice. Does your whole family live here?"

"No."

Okay then...

"What's your full name?"

"Iggy Monroe," I say, and I expect him to write it in my chart or something, but he doesn't move.

"Do you have any siblings?"

"Uh, yeah. Two."

"Older or younger?"

"Older."

"And your parents?"

"What about them?"

"Are they still alive? Do you like them?"

"Yes, and yes."

He nods, and before he can ask any more questions, I interrupt him.

"Am I going to be released soon?"

"No."

"What?"

"I mean, no, not tonight."

"Okay," I say, drawing the word out. "When will I be released?"

"I don't know yet. We'll have to see how a few things heal."

I nod, finishing off my soup and moving on to the pudding.

"Where are you staying?" He asks me.

"With Rue, Bo, and Liam."

He glares when I mention the other men, and I wonder if he's insane.

You're the one attracted to him. So, who is really insane here?

It's true that I can still feel this connection between us. I wonder what that means.

And what I should do about these feelings.

FOUR

Roman

I BARELY SLEPT LAST NIGHT. I was afraid that if I closed my eyes she would disappear, and I would wake up to find out that this was all a dream.

My wolf is content for the first time in a long while. He's been dissatisfied for a long time, and his moodiness was starting to get on my nerves. It's one of the reasons why I was planning an extended vacation to go search for my fated mate.

Now it feels like we're finally back on the same page. He's lying down inside of me, relaxed and happy to just watch over our mate.

Iggy is beautiful. We could sit and watch her for hours, and it's a weird feeling. I'm so used to being go, go, go all the time. I can't remember the last time I sat still for longer than five minutes. Hell, I usually even eat on the go, but now I want to spend all my time with her.

I wonder if she can feel it too. Can she feel the mating

bond between us? Has she noticed the bite mark yet? I had helped her into the bathroom in the middle of the night, but she didn't say anything. I think it was too dark, or maybe she was just still half asleep. I know I'll need to explain it to her soon, though.

I've never thought about how I would explain shifters or fated mates to anyone before. I always assumed that my mate would be a wolf like me or some other kind of animal. They would know about the mating heat and the pull we feel toward our mates, and I wouldn't have to tiptoe around anything. We would both just get it.

That's not going to happen here, and I feel like maybe I already messed up by taking her choice away from her. I am powerless to do anything but love Iggy, but it's not the same for her. That means that I'm going to have to win her over, show her that I can be the perfect partner so that she'll never want to leave me.

My wolf whines inside me at the thought of her rejecting us, and I grit my teeth. *That's not going to happen,* I promise him, and he nods, curling back up inside of me.

The mating moon is in two nights. That means I don't have very long to show her we're meant to be. I can already feel the heat starting between us, and I breathe in deeply, wondering if she can feel it too. It's only going to get stronger from here. Luckily for me, she's healed fast. Biting her saved her life, and now her cuts and scratches have all healed.

Iggy starts to stir in the hospital bed, and I sit up straighter.

Maybe I should leave. Will she think that me watching over her while she sleeps is creepy?

Too late.

"Still here," she says as she wiggles higher in the bed.

"Still here," I confirm, and she eyes me.

"*Why* are you still here?"

Rue! Rue is with two shifters. I could smell them last night. They're best friends. Surely she's told my mate about us.

Relief hits me that I won't have to have this whole conversation from scratch. She'll probably already know most of this.

"We're fated mates," I tell her, and she blinks.

My stomach sinks at her blank look, and I clear my throat.

"Like Bo, Liam, and Rue."

I hate even saying those guys names. They shouldn't have been buying my mate flowers and a teddy bear. I should be the only one taking care of my Iggy.

My wolf growls as we remember how she stared at the flowers. She said they were the first flowers she had ever gotten, and I aim to fix that. I'm going to buy her so many bouquets that she forgets all about the one that Bo gave her.

"What are you talking about?" She asks, and I forget about flowers to focus on this mess that I've created for myself.

"They're shifters, like me. Well, I'm a wolf, and I think they're bears. They smelled like bears anyway," I ramble, and she's looking at me like I'm insane.

"Are you really a doctor?" She blurts out, and I frown.

"Of course I am."

"Prove it," she challenges, and I roll my eyes.

"I saved your life," I remind her, and she rolls her eyes back at me.

"How would I know that it was you? I was unconscious."

"You'll just have to trust me."

"Right. Well, you seem great, but I think that I'd like someone else to take over my care."

"No," I snarl, and she recoils in the bed at my tone.

"Morning," Jax says as he comes into the room.

His hair is still wet, and I know that he must have gone home to shower before coming back for his shift today. I wonder what time he left yesterday. Things were pretty crazy around here for a while, and I lost track of him after he helped me stabilize Iggy.

"Oh, thank God. Can you be my new doctor?" Iggy asks him, and his eyes widen.

"Um..."

"No," I say for him, and Iggy glares at me.

"Don't I get to decide that?"

"No," I say again.

"He's not a real doctor, is he?" Iggy asks Jax, and he looks like he's trying not to laugh.

I glare at him, and he coughs into his hand to hide his smile.

"We're back!" Rue says as she joins us.

Bo and Liam are right behind her, and I try not to glare openly at them as I stand and move closer to her bed.

"Good thing that you're here. This guy is crazy. Can we have him removed?" Iggy asks, and I bare my teeth at Bo and Liam in warning.

"What's going on?" Liam asks with a frown.

"He's crazy! He thinks that you're bears or something!"

Rue, Bo, and Liam all share a look, and Jax stares at me like I'm an idiot.

"We are," Bo says slowly.

"What?" Iggy asks, seeming to deflate in her bed. "Am I dreaming? That must be it."

"No," Rue says, and Jax moves closer to me.

"Are you crazy?" He hisses to me. "You told her that you bit her and forced her to become your fated mate?"

"Not exactly," I hedge.

"You what?!?" Iggy shrieks.

"I did it to save your life," I try to tell her, but she's staring at me with wide eyes.

"You bit me to save my life? Are you crazy?"

"It's true," I tell her, but I can tell that I'm not getting through to her.

My wolf is back to pacing inside me, his agitation about the situation only fueling my own.

"Maybe I should talk to Iggy... alone," Rue says, and I plant my feet.

My wolf and I don't want to leave her, even if we know that Rue and Iggy talking is probably the best thing for us.

"Roman," Jax starts, and I growl.

"Five minutes," I tell them, and Rue nods.

My wolf is snarling in my head, and I grit my teeth.

We'll be back with her in five minutes, I tell him, and we both start to pace as we count down the minutes.

FIVE

Iggy

"WHAT THE HELL IS GOING ON?" I ask Rue as soon as we're alone.

"That's what I wanted to talk to you about yesterday when we went skiing," she says meekly, and I just stare at her.

"Tell me now," I urge, and she nods, taking a seat next to my hospital bed.

I sit up more, throwing my legs over the side of the bed so I can face her. I wish that we weren't having this conversation while I was wearing a hospital gown. It feels like everyone knows what's going on except me, and I don't like it.

"This is... hard to explain, and I didn't believe it when I first heard it. I mean, I barely believed it when Bo and Liam did it in front of me."

"Did what?" I ask, starting to lose patience with everyone.

"Bo and Liam, and I guess Doctor Roman and Doctor Jax, are shifters. They can change between human and an animal. Bo and Liam are bears," she says.

She's explaining it like all of this is completely normal.

"I know that it sounds crazy, but you have to believe me. I can have Bo and Liam shift for you, or I'm sure Roman would do it for you," she rushes to add.

"He would *shift*?" I ask, trying to wrap my head around all of this.

"Yeah, it's actually kind of cool to see," she says with a smile.

"Okay, and why did he bite me?"

"So, they have to bite and mark you to become mates."

I stare at her blankly, and she smiles.

"Shifters have fated mates. It means that they will only love one person."

"But you're with Bo and Liam."

"Yeah, I can love both of them, but they'll only love me. They're destined to only want me. It's actually kind of cool. I never have to worry about them cheating or falling out of love with me. They'll never even look at another girl."

I feel a tug in my core at her words. I want that. I want someone who will only ever want me, who will only ever love me. I want what Rue has with Bo and Liam, but do I really want that with Roman?

Bo and Liam worship the ground Rue walks on. They'd do anything for her. Plus, they're so sweet and laid back.

Roman doesn't seem anything like that. He seems jealous and controlling. He's a doctor too. Don't they work crazy hours? Would we even see each other?

"So, I'm Roman's fated mate?" I ask, and she nods.

"Well, I think so. He bit you, though I think Bo

mentioned once that shifters can force the mating bond by biting someone."

"He's forcing me to be his mate?"

"No, I think you were fated, and you don't have to choose him."

"What happens if I don't choose him?"

"You will," Roman says as he stomps back into the room.

"Aww," Rue says, and I glare at her. "My men can't stand to be away from me either."

"Great," I tell her, and she laughs.

"Get out," I try to order Roman.

"No, you said five minutes. It's been five minutes."

"Can I leave then?"

"You're being discharged today. I'll take you home," Roman says, and I grind my teeth together.

"Rue is here. She can take me home."

"Our home," he clarifies. "I can answer any other questions that you have."

"Are we fated mates, or did you force this?"

"We're fated mates."

"You're a wolf?"

"Yes."

"How do you know that we're meant to be?"

"I can smell it."

"Don't love that, but okay."

"No, it's good. You smell good," he reassures me.

"What happens now?"

"I take you home, we spend a few days together, and hopefully, by the end of the week, you're as in love with me as I am with you."

"You don't know me, so you can't love me," I point out.

"I can, and I do," he argues back.

My brain stalls at that. It seems so crazy that I could go from single to basically married just like that.

"The mating moon is coming up," Jax says, and Roman growls at him.

"The what?"

"We can discuss that later," Roman says. "Let's get you out of that hospital gown."

"That's what I was trying to say," Jax whispers as Roman stalks past him.

"Just give him a chance. We'll be there to pick you up if you need us," Rue tells me, and I sigh as I climb out of the hospital bed.

This trip is not going how I imagined it would, and I'm starting to wonder if that's a good thing or not.

SIX

Roman

IT ONLY TAKES me a few minutes to get Iggy's discharge paperwork in order, but I'm delayed from getting back to her by Jax.

"Dude, you are blowing this."

"No, I'm not. We just need to get out of here and get to know each other better."

"You're pushing her away by being so controlling," he warns me, and my wolf snarls at him.

He doesn't know what he's talking about.

Does he?

"I'll be fine," I assure him as I turn to head back to her room.

Bo, Liam, and Rue are still in Iggy's room, and I try to think of a polite way to tell them to get lost, but I'm saved from having to do that.

"We'll get out of your hair. Call me if you need anything," Rue says as she hugs Iggy goodbye.

I nod goodbye to them, and once we're alone, I pass Iggy her bag of clothes.

"We'll have to go get your things from Rue's. These have some blood on them, so I gave you one of my scrub tops too."

"Thanks," Iggy says as she takes the hospital bag from me.

"I just need you to sign a few papers. It's about your medicine and some aftercare instructions."

"I don't think I need any pain medicine. I really don't feel bad at all," she says, and I nod.

"That's because I bit you. You got some of my shifter qualities when we became mates and were able to heal faster."

"How do you treat your other patients?" She mumbles, and I bite back a laugh.

"Are you jealous, mate?" I ask, and she glares at me.

"I'm not your mate."

"Yet."

We stare at each other for a beat, and she breaks first, grabbing the clothes and disappearing into the bathroom to change. I get the papers ready for her to sign and tuck her medicine bottle into my jacket pocket.

As soon as she signs these, I can turn them in, and we can be on our way. My wolf and I are anxious to finally have our mate in our home. We want her scent all over our things. We want to have her all to ourselves.

My wolf licks his lips. He's practically salivating at the thought of it being just the two of us alone in our bedroom.

The bathroom door opens, and Iggy comes out in my scrub top and her jeans. My top is too big on her, and hangs off one of her shoulders. I wish I could see her curves more, but this way, her bite mark is on full display. The caveman in me loves seeing our mark on her, and my wolf howls at the sight of our brand on her flawless skin.

"Here's the paperwork. It says that you should take it easy for a few days. If you have any pain in your abdomen, come back in immediately. I'll be there, though, and I'll keep an eye on you in case anything happens. You should be good, though."

She nods, taking the pen from me, and our fingers brush. Tingles race down my arm at the contact, and my eyes fly to hers. She staring at me wide-eyed, and I know then that she can feel this connection between us.

"Thanks," she mumbles as she takes the pen and signs the discharge papers.

"Great, now we can head home."

"I really think I should just stay with Rue and the guys."

"Not happening. We'll go get your clothes from their place, but then you'll stay with me."

"Why are you doing this?" She snaps, shoving the papers into my chest. "We don't know each other. I don't love this overbearing attitude. Why do we have to basically become roommates?"

"We're not going to be roommates," I growl. "We're fated to be. I know it, and soon, you're going to admit it too. I know that you can already feel this thing between us."

"Prove it," she snaps.

"I'm going to! You're coming home with me. The mating moon is in two days, and you're going to be begging me to fuck you."

"Not a chance," she snarls back at me.

"Great, then you don't have an issue with staying with me for the next few days. Now, let's go."

I take her hand, dragging her after me as I stomp down the hallway to the front door. We pass Jax, and he shakes his head in disappointment at me. I ignore him, leading Iggy outside and over to my car. I get her door for her, but she ignores me as she slides in.

At least she's in my car.

The drive to my house is filled with icy silence, and when we pull up out front, she tenses even more.

"We were supposed to go to Rue's," she snaps and I grip the steering wheel.

"You should be resting. We can go later to get your things."

She doesn't say anything back to that as she unbuckles her seatbelt.

I live in a modern two-story house close to the center of our pack's land. I had it built after I graduated from medical school and moved back to Aspen Ridge. I had visions of living here with my mate and our pups, and now it's finally happening.

My wolf leaps to his feet inside me. He's so ready for Iggy to be in our space.

"I'll get your door."

"I can open a door."

"Can you also sit there?"

Her head whips my way, and I swallow.

"Sorry. I'm messing this all up."

"You really are," she says, but her tone has softened.

I close my door once more and sigh.

"I've had an image of how this would happen for so long, but it's not going that way. I'm just feeling a little off balance. I've never done any of this before."

"If it makes you feel any better, neither have I," she admits quietly.

My wolf howls when we realize she's telling us she's never been with anyone.

"Let's go inside. I can show you around, make us something to eat, and we can try this again."

She still seems a little wary of me, but when she nods, I know we're headed in the right direction. We both climb out of the car, and I rest my hand on the small of her back as I lead her up to the front door.

"Your house is... really nice. It's not what I pictured for a place in the middle of the woods."

"A lot of people have cabins out here, but this is more my style."

"I like all of the windows."

"Yeah, this place has a great view of the forest and mountains. I didn't want to block that. Do you like the modern style? We can move," I tell her.

She lets out a startled laugh and stares at me like she can't tell if I'm joking or not.

I'm not.

I would do anything to make this girl happy.

"Come on; I'll show you around."

I give her a quick tour, showing her the kitchen, living room, office, and bedrooms. There isn't much to see in most of the rooms. I have a desk and some papers in the office, a bed and dresser in the master bedroom, and a TV and couch in the living room.

"I didn't spend much time on furnishing the place. I figured that my mate would want to do that."

Iggy nods, not saying anything to that, and I wonder if I'm coming on too fast.

"How about I make us something to eat, and we can get to know each other some more."

"Sounds good," Iggy says as she follows me back to the kitchen.

She's not running out of here yet. That's a good sign.

I've still got a chance here.

"What can I help with?" She asks, and my wolf shakes his head. He wants to be the one to take care of her, but I know that my Iggy is stubborn. If I tell her to take a seat, she's going to be mad at me again.

"Why don't you cut up the vegetables while I get the chicken ready?"

She nods, and I pull out a cutting board and knife for her. I put the potatoes next to her, and she starts to slice them as I grab the chicken and green beans from the fridge.

We work together in silence for a few minutes, and my wolf is starting to get impatient inside me. He wants us to be closer to her. He wants to know everything about her so that we can make her happy. Then she'll never want to leave us.

"Do you have any pets?" I blurt out, and the question seems to catch her off guard.

"Uh, apparently, I have a wolf now," she jokes, and I laugh.

"What about back in Anchorage?" I try again.

"No, it's just my parents and me in our house. My brother and sister moved out a few years ago."

"I'm an only kid," I tell her, and she nods as she finishes up the potatoes.

"Are your parents still here in town?"

"No, they moved down south when I left for college."

"Do you see them often?"

"No, I've been so busy with medical school and then getting started at the hospital that I haven't had a ton of time to travel to visit them."

"Do you miss them?"

"Sometimes," I admit. "But I keep busy."

She nods, moving on to the green beans as I slide the chicken and potatoes into the oven.

"What do you do in Anchorage?"

"I work at this coffee shop and then at this little clothing boutique downtown."

"Two jobs?" I ask, and my wolf starts pacing.

He hates that she's working herself to death. We'll fix that now that we've found her. We can take care of everything.

"Yeah, I need the money," she says quietly, and I can tell that this is a sensitive topic for her.

"What was your favorite subject in school," I ask, trying to steer us back to a more neutral topic.

"English," she says with a small smile. "I'm guessing that yours was science?"

"Yep. I loved the experiments," I admit, and she grins at me. "If you could live anywhere, where would it be?"

"Hmm," she hums, thinking it over. "I'm not sure, but I know that it wouldn't be Anchorage," she admits and I file that information away.

"What's your favorite food?"

We spend the next fifteen minutes playing twenty questions. I learn that Iggy's favorite color is blue, her favorite food is pizza, she's always wanted to travel and get out of Anchorage, and that Rue is her best friend and has been since they were young.

All of that is in my favor. She wants to leave her hometown so she can move here and live with me. That way, she's close to Rue too. I'll feed her pizza every day and paint every room in the house blue.

"Ready to eat?" I ask as I take the food out of the oven, and Iggy nods.

She seems a lot more relaxed around me now, and that has to be a good sign. My wolf nods, starting to settle inside me as we sit at the kitchen table.

I smile at her as I pick up my fork, and she smiles back at me.

I could get used to this...

SEVEN

Iggy

"THIS IS the main strip in town," Roman tells me as we head through town.

We're headed over to Rue's place to get my bags. We never got around to it yesterday after dinner. Roman basically fed me, drew me a bath, and tucked me in. He insisted that I needed more rest.

I had worn some more of his clothes to bed, and I'm starting to think he likes seeing me in his things. I had mentioned running over to Rue's place when we first got up this morning, but he had kept making excuses.

Now it's close to four in the afternoon, and we're taking a roundabout way to my friend's house.

"It's a cute town," I comment, and he seems to like my answer.

"Think you can see yourself living here?" Roman asks, and my stomach clenches.

"Um, maybe," I hedge.

He's been doing that a lot. He drops hints about me living here with him in almost every other sentence. Sometimes he catches himself and apologizes. I know he's trying to adjust to this, just like I am.

I had a vision of getting my first boyfriend and dating for a few years before we got married and settled down, but Roman had imagined that he would meet, or I guess smell, his fated mate, and then bam! They would be together forever.

Now, I don't know what will happen. Can I really trust that this is forever? Am I just supposed to be with this guy I met yesterday because he says we're mates or meant to be or whatever?

I need to talk to Rue again. She was more skeptical than I am, so if she could get on board with all of this, then maybe I can too.

"It's not as busy or big as Anchorage, but I hope you like it here. My pack is here, but we can move if you want to. I just want you to be happy."

Nerves start to eat at me, and I try to push away my anxiety.

"Your pack?"

"Oh, yeah, Aspen Ridge is a shifter pack. It's a lot of land, so it's divided up into four quadrants. The North Pack, East Pack, South Pack, and West Pack."

"Which are you part of?"

"West. Same as Rue."

"Are there different rules or something for each pack?"

"Some, but the big ones are the same. Don't shift in front of humans, no killing on pack land, no stealing, and all that."

"Have you always belonged to the pack, then?"

"Yeah, my parents were members, and I was born into

it. I left to go to school, but always wanted to come back here."

We start to head away from town, and I recognize some of the houses from when I drove to Rue's house.

"You can just drop me off if you want. I have my car here, and I can drive back," I tell him as we pull up in front of their house.

"I'll wait."

"Don't trust me to come back?" I ask as I climb out of his car.

"Just don't want you to get lost."

I eye him, wondering if that's really it. Somehow, I doubt it.

"Hey, how are you feeling?" Rue asks as she comes out onto the porch.

Her eyes bounce back and forth between us as she looks for clues on how our relationship is doing and I smile at her.

"I'm fine, I promise," I tell her. "I don't need anyone hovering over me."

I give Roman a pointed look, and he rolls his eyes at me.

"So, I see that you two are doing good," Bo says with a laugh as he opens the door for us.

"We're fine," Roman tells them in a hard tone, and I glare at him.

"Be nice," I hiss.

He sighs but nods as we head inside.

"Your bags are still up in your room," Liam tells me.

"We can grab them," Bo offers, and Roman growls.

"I'll get her things."

"No, *I'll* get my things," I snap at him, and Rue giggles as she follows me up the stairs.

"How are things really going?" She asks once we're alone.

"I don't know. It's a lot to take in. How did you wrap your head around all of this?"

"Well, I was trapped with them," she says, and I laugh.

"So, you're saying I should be praying for a snowstorm or something so I'm stranded with him?"

"It might help?"

"The sad thing is that I think if I mentioned that to Roman, he would start shoveling snow or finding some other way to trap me in his house."

"Is that a bad thing? That he would do anything for you?" She asks quietly, and I chew on my bottom lip.

"I don't know. This is all just too much."

"I felt the same way, but things got better when I just let myself go with the flow. I wasn't trying to plan my future or control anything. I just followed my heart, which I know is super cliché, but it worked out for the best."

"I want what you have with Bo and Liam," I admit, and she smiles.

"I want that for you too. I've never been happier. I know that my guys would do anything for me. They love me more than life itself and love spoiling me. It's hard not to fall in love with that."

"Roman isn't quite as... sweet as Bo and Liam," I admit, and she laughs.

"I've noticed. He comes on a bit strong, but I know that he means well. A lot of shifters have been searching for their fated mates for years. He might have thought that it would never happen for him, and now he's got to be terrified that you're going to leave or reject him."

"So, what do you suggest I do?"

"Give yourself a time limit. Tell him that you want him to show you what being his mate would be like without the pressure of you leaving hanging over his head. If you hate it, then at least you tried, and you can go back to Anchorage and get on with your life."

"And if I do like it?"

"Then you've found your soulmate. There's no downside."

"I can't stay here, Rue. I have to go home and help out my family."

She nods, looking sad.

"What if you got a job here and sent money home? That might even be better because they wouldn't have to pay for your food or utilities and all of that," she says, perking up.

"That's true."

I mull over her words as I grab my bag, and we head back downstairs. As soon as I'm halfway down the stairs, Roman is there to grab my bag from me, and I take a deep breath.

"Time limit," Rue whispers to me, and I sigh but nod.

"I have to head back to Anchorage in a few days. That will have to be it."

Rue squeezes my hand and pulls me into a hug.

"I'll be here if you need anything."

We hug once more, and I wave at Bo and Liam as I head outside. Roman is stowing my bag in the trunk, and he heads my way as I come down the front porch steps.

"I can come back for your car later if you want to ride with me," he offers, and I stop on the last step.

We're close to eye to eye now, and I put my hands on my shoulders, leaning up on my tiptoes and pressing my lips against his.

His eyes are wide as I pull back and he seems thrown off by my actions.

"What was that for? Not that I'm complaining!" He rushes to add.

"Rue said something. That I should give this a chance, and I think maybe she's right. This isn't how I imagined dating and all that would go, but I don't want to just toss this chance aside either."

"Good, I'm glad," he says, and for the first time since I've met him, he gives me a real smile.

His green eyes light up, and he wraps his arms around my waist, tugging me against his chest.

"I'm going to drive myself back. I'll follow you," I say, and he nods.

He seems hesitant as he leans forward and presses his lips against mine. His kiss is just as quick as mine, and I smile slightly as he pulls back.

"I'll follow you," I tell him again, and he nods.

He takes my hand and leads me over to my car, getting my door for me, and I smile as I slip behind the wheel.

"Brr! The seats are freezing," I say, hurrying to start the engine and crank the heat.

"Drive my car back. It's already warm," he says, and before I can argue, he's dragging me from my old hatchback and leading me over to his.

"It's fine," I say, but he shakes his head.

"My car is better on the snow-covered roads anyway. It's safer."

My heart thumps loudly in my ears. It feels good to have him care about me and my safety. I can see what Rue was talking about. Having Roman's undivided attention is intoxicating.

My parents have been too worried about keeping the family afloat and paying the bills to pay much attention to me. I know they love me and are trying their best, but it's been a while since we really connected or checked in with each other.

The leather seat in Roman's car is warm and supple beneath my legs and I wiggle my butt deeper into the seat.

Just try to be with him, I remind myself as I follow him out onto the road.

Maybe I could get used to this after all.

EIGHT

Roman

IGGY SAID she loved pizza so I went all out for our second date. Well, maybe not date, but dinner. My wolf and I are calling it a date, though.

I set the pasta and garlic bread on the table next to the homemade pizza. It took me three tries to get the dough right, but I'm pleased with how it came out this time. I just hope that my mate likes it too.

My wolf snaps at me. He's hungry for something more than food. The mating heat is pressing down on us already, and I know this is my chance to really win Iggy over. I'm not sure that my wolf and I can survive until next month to claim her.

The front door opens, and I take a deep breath, trying to calm my wolf and me down as I go to greet my girl.

"It smells so good in here," she says as she shrugs out of her jacket.

"I cooked us dinner," I tell her, and she smiles.

"Bo and Liam did the same for Rue. It must be in the air or something because they sure were in a hurry for me to leave," she says with a laugh, and I swallow hard.

I'm going to have to tell her more about shifters and the mating moon, and I'm not sure how she's going to take it.

She's wearing a tight pair of yoga pants and a loose-fitting sweater that hangs off one shoulder, exposing my bite mark. My eyes zero in on the length of her neck that is now exposed, and I wonder if I should say I'm not feeling well and go lay down. Or more like barricade myself in my bedroom. No way can I make it through tonight with her looking like that. Especially if she rejects me.

Coward, my wolf snarls, and I sigh.

"Did you want to go out to dinner instead?" I croak.

"What? No, it smells really good, and I'm starving. Wait, are you feeling alright?" She asks, stepping closer to me with a look of concern on her face.

This is my chance. Say no and leave or tell her all about the mating heat.

"You don't look so well," she says, stepping closer to me and resting her hand on my forehead. "You feel really hot. Why don't you go lay down?"

"No, I'm fine."

"You don't look fine," she says, looking skeptical.

"It's not an illness. It's the mating heat."

"That what?" She asks, and I take her hand, leading her into the kitchen.

"Let's eat. I'll tell you about it over dinner."

"Alright," she says, and I hurry to pull out her chair.

I take the one next to her and try to discreetly wipe the sweat from my brow as I start to fill her plate with food.

"Are you sure that you're okay?" She asks, eyeing me carefully.

"I'm sure. It's the full moon tonight," I start. "And that means that every mated shifter is going to feel the mating heat."

"What's that?"

"It's... it's pure desire."

Her fork clatters to her plate, and she stares at me with wide eyes.

"I always wanted you, but tonight, it's going to feel like I'll die if I don't have you."

She still doesn't say anything to that, and I rush to clarify.

"I'm not trying to pressure you! We'll only do what you're comfortable with. We'll go at your pace."

"Right," she says, and she looks like she's in a bit of a daze.

We eat in silence for a few minutes, but I notice that Iggy is really just pushing her food around her plate.

"Do you want something else to eat?" I ask, and she shakes her head.

"I'm fine. This is really good. Thanks for cooking for me."

"I didn't mean to freak you out."

"I know, but it's still so hard for me to wrap my head around all of this."

"Would it help if I... well, if I shifted for you? Maybe if you see my wolf, it will make it real?"

She chews on her bottom lip, her eyes filled with curiosity, and finally, she nods.

"Okay, let's do it."

I leave the food on the table as I stand, taking Iggy's hand and leading her down the hall to my bedroom. It feels like I'm hoping for too much to do this in here, but my wolf and I both think it feels right.

"How do we do this?" Iggy asks, and she seems just as nervous as I am.

"I need to take my clothes off."

"This would be a really weird pick up line," she says, and I let out a surprised laugh.

"It would. It's not a pick up line, though. I promise."

She nods, and I reach for the back of my shirt, tugging it over my head and dropping it at my feet. My hands reach for the button on my jeans, and I look at Iggy to make sure that she's still alright with this.

Her eyes are locked on my chest, and my wolf preens when he realizes she's turned on by what she sees.

Maybe we're not the only ones feeling the mating heat today.

I push my jeans and boxers down my thighs and then take a deep breath.

"Are you ready?"

"Uh-huh," she says distractedly.

Her eyes are locked on my cock, which is rapidly lengthening as her gaze heats with lust. Having her staring at us like that is a major turn-on, and my wolf snaps.

Claim her! He screams in my head, and I grit my teeth.

Behave or she'll run out of here and we'll never see her again, I remind him.

I nod, meeting her gaze as I let my wolf push through. My hair, nails, and teeth start to grow, and in seconds, I'm landing on my paws in front of her.

She gasps, her eyes wide as she stares at me. It's like she's frozen as she watches my wolf and I take a tentative step forward.

"It's a lot bigger than I thought," she says quietly, and she seems a little nervous.

I remain still, letting her come to me when she's ready.

It takes a few minutes, but she takes a tentative step toward me and then another. Her hand reaches out and she strokes her fingers through my fur.

My wolf is practically purring as her hands move over me, and I lean against her legs. I'm enjoying her attention, but when she steps back, I know it's time to shift back and see where we stand.

I shift back, grabbing the sheet off the bed and wrapping it around my waist.

"Now what?" She asks, and I swallow.

"That's up to you. I know that shifters and fated mates are all new to you, and you probably don't believe me when I say that we're meant to be, but—"

"I do," she says, cutting me off.

"You do?"

"Yeah, I can't really explain it, but I trust you."

"Good, that's good."

She stares at me, and I take a deep breath, trying to calm my wolf down. He's pacing back and forth inside me. We're so close to finally fully claiming her that we can taste it.

I take a deep breath and when I can smell her desire, I know I might actually have a chance to pull this off.

"What's next?" She asks.

"Well, I've already bit you, so the next part would be claiming you."

"You mean sex."

"Yes," I say hoarsely, nodding slowly.

She nods, her eyes locking with mine. I'm not sure who moves first, but soon, we're wrapped around each other. I let the sheet drop and lift her in my arms so that I can attack her mouth with mine.

"Iggy, God," I groan once she breaks our kiss to gulp down air. "I never want you to think I'm just using you for your body, and if this is too fast for you, then let me know, but I need my lips on your skin, need to taste you, need to feel more of you," I tell her truthfully. "I *ache* for you, mate."

She nods, and I can see the desperate edge in her eyes. She's trying to play it cool, but she wants me just as much as I want her. She's stronger than me when it comes to the mating pull, that's for damn sure, but my mate needs to come too.

Iggy bites her bottom lip, drawing my eyes to that spot. My dick lengthens even more, pressing against her pussy through her yoga pants. I hold my breath, waiting for her response. I'll never take what she doesn't freely give, but Jesus, I really need her to say yes.

Finally, she nods her head and lets out a breathy whimper of need.

I'm on her in the next breath, moving us over to the bed, laying her on her back, pinning her arms above her head, and nudging her legs wider.

"Are you aching for me, mate?" I all but growl.

I need to hear that she wants me as much as I need her. She nods, her pupils dilating and cheeks flushing. So damn beautiful.

I grunt and slam my mouth down over hers, swallowing her moans of pleasure as I thrust my tongue in and out of her sweet lips. Iggy wriggles underneath me, and I release her arms, freeing up both of my hands to roam over her body.

We break apart, gasping for air as I help her sit up and peel off her shirt. My eyes lock on the scar on her chest and we both freeze.

"Oh, yeah... I had heart surgery when I was a baby. They had to fix a valve," she says, trying to cover herself up.

I mover her hands out of the way, leaning forward and softly kissing the old scar tissue.

"Perfect," I whisper against her skin and I look up to meet her eyes.

She looks so vulnerable, and my heart threatens to burst out of my chest. My wolf whines. He wants to lick the scar, to lick all of her, and I push him down and get back to worshipping my mate.

My hands run up and down the smooth skin of her stomach, her ribs, and then cup her perfect breasts still covered in a lace bra. I rub my thumbs over her already hard nipples, making her moan and arch her back. I deftly unhook her bra and slide it down her arms before bending down and sucking one perky tit into my mouth.

"Oh fuck me," she whispers, tipping her head back and tangling her fingers in my hair.

"I aim to, mate."

I smile with a mouthful of her breast and bite down gently on her nipple. Iggy's whole body jerks, making me completely ravenous for her.

Back and forth I suck, lick, nibble, and knead her tender flesh, and she loves every second. I think I could make her come just like this, but I have other plans for her. I pop off her tit, making her whimper and pout. Grinning, I scoot down between her legs and hook my thumbs into her yoga pants and panties.

"Still okay?" I grunt, needing her permission even though I might die if I don't have her taste on my tongue in the next three seconds.

"Yes!" She gasps out, and I grin.

I groan in approval and start tugging her pants and panties down, slowly revealing the curve of her hips.

She takes a breath like she's going to say something, but

then I pull her pants all the way down, baring her ripe, juicy cunt to me for the first time. I rid her of the last scraps of clothing and then take my time looking her up and down from my position on my knees in front of her.

I don't have it in me to draw this out any longer. Scooting down her body, I throw her legs over my shoulders and dive into that pussy. I flatten my tongue and lick from her entrance up to her clit. As soon as I tap her tight bundle of nerves, Iggy erupts.

"FUCK!" She screams, her thighs clamping down on my head, her back bowed off the mattress, her fingers clawing the sheets as her orgasm rips through her.

I don't stop. Not for a second.

Using my tongue, my lips, and my teeth, I keep stimulating her throbbing clit, pushing her past her orgasm, higher, higher, higher, till she's shaking, gasping for air, pleading for me to give her mercy. Only then do I ease off her over-sensitive bundle of nerves and turn my attention to lapping up her release.

Iggy shudders as I gently bring her down with long, steady strokes of my tongue, licking her clean.

I place her legs back bed and crawl on top of her, holding myself up with a forearm on either side of her head. I stare down at my mate as she opens her eyes and looks at me with such awe. I can't explain what that does to me. I've never felt anything like it, having her admiration, seeing her like this, knowing I put that look there.

"More," she whispers while rocking her hips and gliding her pussy up and down the underside of my aching cock.

My curvy mate is gorgeous. Too damn beautiful for me, that's for sure. But she's mine anyway and I'm not letting her go. I can't now that I've finally found her.

Iggy chews on her lip nervously, and I realize I've just

been drooling over her flawless skin and decadent curves. I know without her saying that she's a virgin. That thought makes me growl and my wolf goes crazy, needing to be the only one inside of her. We'll only ever belong to each other.

"You're perfect," I whisper, though all I want to do is roar and devour every inch of her. She deserves better, though.

My cock nudges against her snug opening, and I grit my teeth as I move against her. I fist her hair and tug, giving me access to her tempting little mouth. My lips crash down on hers, and we lose ourselves in each other's passion.

"Roman!" she says, her tone indicating she's been saying my name for a little while now. I can't help it; I'm just so lost in her.

"Hm?"

"I need you," she pleads, and I nod eagerly.

"Iggy..."

She cuts me off by leaning up and capturing my lips in a scorching kiss. I growl into her mouth and take over her movements, sliding my dick up and down her wet pussy, but never entering her. She gives in so beautifully to me, trusting me with her body, her pleasure. Back and forth, I rub my swollen fucking cock over her sensitive bundle of nerves until she's panting again.

"Roman, please," she begs, and I can't take it any longer.

I love teasing her, but I'm close to coming all over her, and I need to be inside of her when we come for the first time together. I rub back and forth, my dick pinned between my stomach and her pussy, grinding hard, gritting my teeth against the urge to come.

"I'm going to make this so good for you," I promise her, and she nods.

"I trust you."

I start to push into her, and she tenses slightly as I reach her virginity. My wolf is howling in my head, his lust and excitement heightening my own.

"It will only hurt this first time," I say, kissing her as I thrust fully into her, making her mine.

My wolf growls in my head, and I realize I'm growling out loud too. My balls are tingling and I feel my cock hardening even more as I start to pound into her. I should go slower, but I can't seem to make myself slow down.

I've been on edge for too long, and now that I'm finally with her, I can't control myself anymore.

"So beautiful. So damn tight. Fucking dream come true," I grunt out with each thrust, and Iggy moans, arching against me and taking me deeper.

Her tits are smashed up against my chest, and I feel the hard little peaks rubbing against me with each movement. I'm close to coming already, and I know that I won't last much longer so I bow my head, running my lips over the bite mark on her shoulder.

"Roman!" She shouts as her pussy contracts around my cock and she starts to come.

Her release triggers my own, and I groan into her neck as I follow her over the edge. I chant her name as my come splashes against her womb, and my wolf licks his lips as he thinks about breeding her tonight.

"Mine. Mate," I breathe out against her lips, and she smiles, still breathing hard as I roll us over so that she's sprawled on top of me.

I rest my forehead on hers, breathing in her sugary, fruity scent mixed with our lust. It's intoxicating. It's all I want to smell for the rest of my life, and as I gather her in my arms, I smile, knowing that I finally have my mate.

NINE

Iggy

THE ROOM IS STILL DARK when I slowly open my eyes the next morning. The mattress is so comfy under me, and I burrow further under the blankets and against Roman's side as I wake up a little more

My body is sore, and I'm reminded of all of the things that Roman and I did together last night. That feeling, the pulsing connection between us, is still there today, though it's faded some. I wonder if the mating heat has finally passed now.

I stretch, trying to ease the tenderness in my muscles as I blink the sleep from my eyes. Something is poking me in the back, and it takes me a second to realize what it is.

"Mate," Roman says, his voice groggy still.

I grind back against his thick erection, loving the way it makes him tremble with need.

"Easy," he grits out, his hand gripping my hip tighter.

"You don't want me?" I ask, rolling over to face Roman.

His dark green eyes glow in the dim light, his pulse starting to race the longer he stares at me. Finally, he moves, leaning forward and capturing my lips with his. I moan softly as he growls and slides his hands over my naked body.

My skin prickles with awareness everywhere he touches me. The heat I felt last night is back, threatening to burn me alive, and I move, throwing my leg over his waist and straddling him so that I can feel him where I need him most.

I can't help the needy whimper that falls from my lips when my bare pussy rubs up against his cock. I feel him lengthen and harden beneath me, the sensation making me so, *so* wet.

I wrap my arms around his neck and hold him close as I grind down on his lap. Roman groans and breaks our kiss, only for his lips to start to nibble down my neck. I shiver and squeeze my thighs around his hips, needing more.

"Please," I beg, and he moans.

"I'll give you anything that you want, mate."

Roman leans back and cups my face, resting his forehead on mine. We're both breathing heavily, the air thick with what we both crave. He slides his hands down my neck, shoulders, and torso until he cups my ass, squeezing the soft flesh in a possessive hold.

I feel vulnerable and yet somehow bold. His fingertips trail up my sides in featherlight touches as he looks at me with a mix of awe and reverence. He's looking at me like I'm the center of his world, and it's addictive.

Leaning forward, Roman captures one of my nipples in his mouth, gently sucking as his hands slide around to my back, pressing me closer to him. I tip my head back and rock my hips against his, savoring every swipe of his tongue and stroke of his fingers.

Roman hums in approval as I grind against him faster,

and he switches breasts, lavishing the other with the same attention. I feel the vibrations deep down in my core, making more of my arousal drip down and coat his hot, throbbing dick. I feel it swell up even more as a soft growl rumbles up from his chest.

I slide my hands down his sculpted chest, pushing him back. He grunts in frustration like I took away his favorite toy, and it makes me giggle knowing he wants me that much.

Roman looks up at me with the softest smile, making me melt for him; even while I'm so turned on, I feel like I might burst into flames at any second.

"Fuck, I love that sound. Love every single time I can get you to laugh or smile at me."

God, how is this man so freaking perfect? He really is my perfect match.

I don't know how to respond to him with words, so I kiss him once again as my hands trail lower, lower, lower, until my fingers wrap around his cock, stroking him and rubbing his precum up and down his thickness.

"Jesus, Iggy," he grunts, his muscles tensing and flexing as I pick up my pace. Roman grips my hips and lifts me up, positioning me so the head of his cock is right at my entrance. My core clenches up and releases more of my wetness, helping him to slide in easily. "This what you need, mate? Need me to fill you up? You could have just asked."

"Yes! God, Roman," I breathe out, moaning as my tight channel stretches to accommodate him.

I feel every vein and ridge of his shaft as he enters me. It feels so damn good to be connected like this, to be filled so completely in a way that only Roman can provide.

Roman groans and sucks on the bite mark on my neck as

his hands slide up my back and grip my shoulders. He presses my body down on his as he grinds his thick cock against me, hitting my clit just right with each pass.

I jerk and tremble in his embrace, gasping for air when he pushes me right to the edge. Roman trails his fingers back down my spine, gripping my ass and spreading my cheeks apart as he starts to fuck up into my drenched cunt.

"Love feeling you dripping for me, Iggy. Love your sexy fucking body," he murmurs, nipping at my earlobe and causing me to shudder in his arms.

"Oh God," is all I can manage to say, too lost in the sensation of his cock scraping along my walls and hitting every pleasure point inside of me.

I feel my orgasm starting to form deep in my core, throbbing outward and seizing up my muscles. My joints lock up, and I suck in a breath, bracing myself for what's to come. I squeeze my core around him and roll my hips in jerky motions, needing to come so bad it hurts.

Roman senses my urgency, cupping the back of my neck and drawing me down for a passionate kiss. He pulls my bottom lip through his teeth before diving in, tangling his tongue with mine as he bounces me on his length. He tilts his hips and hits that one spot that drives me crazy. Over and over, he hammers into me until the coil snaps, and I cry out my orgasm. Pure pleasure slams into me, overwhelming my senses as I writhe and whimper and get completely swept away by my release.

"We need to get you cleaned up," Roman says, and I groan as he pulls me from the bed and carries me into the shower.

I'm still in a haze as we step under the hot water, and I let Roman take control. He lets me lean against him as he washes my hair, the suds running down my body.

By the time he turns the water off, I'm back to my usual self, and I wrap a towel around my body as I head into the closet in search of my duffle bag. I grab a pair of yoga pants and a sweater, tugging them on as Roman gets dressed behind me.

It feels so weird to be naked and doing things like this with him, but it also feels natural. I'm at ease with him now, and I wonder if that's part of this whole shifter mate thing too.

Roman pulls me into his arms and frowns down at me.

"What's wrong?" I ask him.

"I need to go to work," Roman says apologetically, and I smile as his grip on me tightens.

"When will you be home?"

"It's an eight-hour shift. As long as there are no emergencies, I should be home just after six."

"Sounds good," I say, and he drops a quick kiss on my lips.

"What are you going to do today? Go see Rue for a little bit?"

"Yeah, I feel bad that I came out here to see her and I've barely spent any time with her."

"Do you want me to drive you over there before I go to the hospital? The roads are still snowy."

"I'll be fine."

"I'll leave you my car. It's safer."

"Roman, I'll be fine. I promise."

He frowns but finally relents. He's been working hard on letting me have my way, and I appreciate it. I can see how hard it is for him. He can't stand the idea of me not being safe, and part of me loves it, but I've gotten enough of that in my life from my parents.

"I'll call you on my lunch break," he promises, and I

nod, letting him kiss me once more before he heads out to his car.

I watch him drive off and head back inside to get dressed. His house feels so cold and lifeless without him here. I know he said I could add anything I wanted and that this would be our place, but I have no idea about interior design. I would hate to mess up his place.

I dig through my duffle bag for something warm to wear. I haven't messaged Rue yet to see if she wants to hang out. She's messaged me a few times, but I haven't really gotten a chance to respond to her yet.

I pull my thick wool sweater over my head and then go in search of my phone. Roman must have plugged it in for me because it's on his nightstand. I unplug it and my phone starts to ring. It's my mom, and for one brief second, I consider not answering. I know that she's not going to have anything that I want to hear right now. Lately, she's only called me if she needs something.

I'm a terrible daughter.

Guilt eats at me, and I answer the phone before it can go to voicemail.

"Hey, mom. Is everything okay?"

How sad is it that that's how I answer her phone calls now?

"Yes, dear. I was just calling to see how your trip was going. You don't want to come home early or anything?"

She sounds strained, and I know that it has to be money problems. It's always money problems.

"Um, I can if you need me to."

Just saying the words has the bite mark on my neck aching, and I wish I could take them back.

"We just... we're a little short this month, dear."

"It's okay, mom. I can come home today and pick up some shifts this week."

"Are you sure?" She asks, but she sounds so relieved, and I know I can't say no.

"I'm sure."

"We'll see you soon then, honey."

"See you."

I end the call and look around the sparsely furnished bedroom. I can't believe I let myself get wrapped up in this fantasy. What was I going to do? Move here? Live with Roman, a guy that I just met?

How could I even think of abandoning my family when they've done so much for me?

My mom calling was a good thing. This whole relationship is moving too fast. It was just a fling, and I let myself get wrapped up in it, but it could never last.

The lies I'm telling myself don't help, and I sigh, sinking down on the edge of the bed.

What should I do? Who do I choose?

I don't want to leave Roman or Aspen Ridge. I don't know when or how, but I've fallen in love with my grumpy shifter doctor. He's so sweet to me. I know he would do anything for me, and even though all of this shifter and fated mates stuff is new to me, I trust it. The two of us, we're meant to be.

On the other hand, though, I'm the reason my family is struggling. I owe it to them to go back. Maybe I can try to find a job in Aspen Ridge and move back here, but for right now, I need to make money and help my family. I can't let them down.

I try to hold back the tears as I pack up my things. Roman had tried to unpack them for me this morning, and I have to double-check that I have everything.

What do I do now? Should I call him and tell him that I'm leaving? He probably won't see it for hours, and I don't want to fight with him right now. I need to go home, and he'll have to understand that.

In the end, I leave a note, pinning it to the fridge where I know he'll see it before I carry my things to the car. If we're really meant to be, then we'll find another way back to each other.

Right?

My heart is breaking as I climb behind the wheel and start to head home. My heart is what got my family into this mess, though, and I'm not letting it do any more damage to them.

I try to hold off the tears as I drive down the backroads toward the highway, but by the time I turn on cruise control, I've lost the battle.

Why does it feel like I've just made the biggest mistake of my life?

TEN

Roman

"WHAT'S WRONG?" Jax asks as he rushes into the cafeteria and steals half of my sandwich.

"I've been trying to call Iggy, but she's not answering."

"She's probably busy with her friend," he says with an easy shrug.

"I guess. It still just feels... off."

My wolf is pacing back and forth inside me. He wants us to leave now and go find her. I won't be able to focus on anything except where she is and if she's okay, but my lunch break is almost over.

We've been slammed today, and it's a miracle that I haven't been paged back to the emergency room already.

"Why don't you try to call her friend and see if she's still there?" Jax suggests.

"I don't have her number. I didn't think to get it."

"Rookie mistake," Jax says, shaking his head at me as he shoves the rest of the sandwich into his mouth.

"I know. Do you happen to have Bo or Liam's numbers?"

"No, sorry."

He grabs my chips next, and I shove the tray toward him so he can help himself. My wolf is restless inside of me. He snarls, urging me to get out of here.

Our pagers go off at the same time and we both groan as we stand to head back to the emergency room floor.

Being so busy is both a blessing and a curse. It forces me to push away my worries and unease and focus on my patients. It also means that the time seems to rush by, and soon I'm clocking out.

"Good luck with your mate," Jax says as we walk to our cars.

"Thanks," I say distractedly.

My wolf is a mess inside of me. He wants out so that he can run home, and part of me wants that too. Maybe I can burn off some of this stress and anxiety.

There are too many people around, I remind him, and he growls at me. *We'll talk to her, make her promise to always have her phone on her, and then fuck all of this energy out.*

I speed on the icy roads all the way home. When I don't see her car in the driveway, I turn right back around and head over to Rue's house. Her car isn't parked outside their place either, but I still park and head up to the front door.

Maybe she just left. I could have just missed her.

My wolf is half out of his mind with worry and panic. It's getting harder and harder to hold him back. I raise my nose to the air, trying to catch my Iggy's scent but there's nothing here.

I knock on the front door, pacing back and forth along the porch as I wait for someone to answer.

"Roman?" Rue asks, and both of her mates are right behind her.

"Yeah, is Iggy here?"

"No, I haven't seen her in a few days. I thought that she was with you?" Rue says with a frown.

"She was. I had to go to work today, and she said she might come over here."

"Maybe she went to town to grab something," Rue says, but she doesn't look convinced by her own words.

"Maybe. I'll try to call her again."

Rue nods, and I turn, heading back to the car. I race all the way home, calling Iggy's phone again and again but she never picks up.

My teeth and nails start to elongate as I slowly lose my skin. I slam on the brakes as I pull up in front of the house and sprint inside. My wolf is sniffing the air as we run through the house. She's not in the bedroom or living room. I skid to a halt in the kitchen when my eyes lock on the note on the fridge.

I know before I read it that I'm not going to like what she wrote. My wolf is howling in my head, and it's all that I can hear as I scan her words.

ROMAN,

I'M SORRY, please don't be mad, but I have to go.

X.

Iggy

. . .

DON'T BE MAD? *Don't be mad! Is she crazy? I'm pissed! Why did she have to go?*

My wolf is pressing me to go find her and drag her back here. I text her, telling her to call me, but I can't wait for that.

"Maybe she'll answer Rue's call," I mumble to myself as I jog back to my car and peel out of the driveway.

I make it back to Rue's house in record time, and she opens the door before I can even knock.

"She wasn't there?" She asks, and I shake my head.

"No, and she's not answering my calls. Can you try?"

"Yeah."

She pulls out her phone, and I wait impatiently as she pulls up Iggy's phone number and hits dial. She puts it on speakerphone, and my heart races, my wolf angrily pacing back and forth inside me as we wait. It rings twice, and I hold my breath as the call connects and Iggy finally answers.

"Hey, Rue. Sorry, I meant to call you," she says, and she sounds tired.

"It's okay. Are you alright? Where are you?" Rue asks.

"I'm fine. I went home. I have to deal with some family stuff. I'm actually just pulling up to the house now. Can I call you tomorrow?"

Rue looks at me, and my tongue is glued to the top of my mouth. I don't know what to say.

Do I beg her to come back here? Would she? Why didn't she tell me that she had to leave? What's going on with her family?

"Well," Rue says as she ends the call, and I realize that I zoned out for the last part of their conversation.

"What?"

"What are you waiting for? Go get your girl," Rue orders, and it snaps me out of the fog.

"Thanks, Rue," I tell her honestly, and she smiles.

"Good luck. Bring my friend back here. I miss her."

"Me too," I whisper as I head back to my car to go find my mate.

ELEVEN

Iggy

HAS it really only been twenty-four hours since I left Roman and Aspen Ridge? It feels like it's been years. Time passes so slowly without him here with me.

I managed to pick up a shift today at the boutique, and I glance at the clock. I've been here for three hours already, and have another five to go. I sigh as I watch the second hand of the clock slowly tick by.

I had gotten back to Anchorage in the early afternoon and come home to an empty house. Both of my parents were at work and I had never felt so alone. There wasn't any food in the house, and I had looked in all the cabinets. It was in one, tucked in the back, that I found the stack of bills and overdue notices.

Things are even worse than I had thought. There were so many credit card bills, some even in my name, though I had never seen the cards. I'm still not sure how to feel about that.

When I started looking closer at the credit card statements and other bills, I had gotten a pit in my stomach. Or I guess I should say another pit in my stomach since I've had one there already since I drove away from Roman's place. There were charges on there for food delivery and hotels. I know that my parents are allowed to enjoy themselves a little bit, but it still sucks that I'm giving up my life and working two jobs to help with debt when they seem to just be adding to it.

I haven't brought up any of this with my parents just yet, but I know I'll need to. It's starting to eat at me. I've been feeling guilty for our money problems for so long, but I'm starting to wonder if maybe I wasn't the sole cause of all of this.

A dark-haired man passes by the front windows as I rework one of the displays, and my heart lodges in my throat. He turns, and I let out a deep breath when I see it's not Roman.

I've been ignoring his calls and texts since I left. I'm sure he's pissed at me and maybe he's realized that he's better off without me. That would explain why he stopped calling today.

My fingers brush against the bite mark on my neck and a shiver runs through me. I've been doing that a lot. Touching the mark, staring at it in the mirror. It's like I need the reminder that it was real and I didn't just dream it all up.

"Can you fold that table?" Sharon asks as she walks by carrying a box.

"Sure thing," I tell my boss.

I try to push thoughts of Roman from my head as I get back to work, but it's no use. He's all that I can think about. I miss him so much. I wish things could have been different between us. I wish I could have stayed in Aspen Ridge with him, but I can't just abandon my family.

The bell above the door tinkles, and I paste on a smile, turning to greet the newest customer.

"Welcome to—" My voice trails off as my eyes lock with Roman's.

He looks exhausted, with dark circles under his green eyes. When our eyes lock, his gaze turns almost feral. I've never seen him look more animalistic before in my life and goosebumps rise on my arms.

"We need to talk," Roman states plainly, and I swallow hard.

"I left a note," I say lamely, and he glares at me, his canines showing.

"I got your note," he spits out as he stalks toward me.

"Sharon, I'm going to take my break now," I call, and the older woman nods, her eyes wide as she looks between us.

Roman takes my hand and leads me to the back hallway. The store is empty right now so we have some privacy, but my eyes still dance around the space. I'm too afraid to look at him. I know I hurt him and hate that I've caused him pain. I just don't see any way to make everyone happy.

"Why did you run?" Roman asks, his voice sounding broken.

"I had to come home. I have work and my parents here."

"We have enough money that you don't need to work. You should be relaxing at home. *Our* home. We could have come back to visit your parents together."

"It's... it's more than that," I say softly, and he frowns.

"What's holding you here?"

"A debt," I admit.

"What debt? I'll clear it."

"Remember how I told you about my heart surgery?" I

ask with a sigh, and he nods. "Well, it ruined my family. It bankrupted them. I need to work to help support them. They could lose everything."

"That's not on you. Your parents chose that, they saved you, but they have other options. If they really filed for bankruptcy then those debts would have been cleared," he points out, and I bite my bottom lip.

"I can't leave them with nothing."

"So, you're going to give them your life?"

"I don't know," I say, the tears starting to spill onto my cheeks.

"You deserve to be happy," Roman whispers as he pulls me into his arms, and I twist my fingers in his shirt and cling to him.

"It's hard to even think about leaving them. I love them. I don't want them to struggle."

"Let me give them some money. They can pay off their debts, and you can be with me."

"I can't let you do that! It's so much money," I say miserably.

"You can."

"No," I say stubbornly, and he sighs.

"Then I can move here. I'll get a job at one of the hospitals around here."

"But your pack!" I say and then realize that my voice has risen.

I clear my throat, and his grip on me tightens.

"I need you more than I need a pack, Iggy."

"But you built a life there," I try to argue.

"*You* are my life, mate. I love you. I need you. As long as I have you, then I'll be happy."

Part of me is still surprised that he would give up his life like that, no hesitation, no nothing, but I supposed that I shouldn't be. He has been telling me and showing me from the beginning how much I mean to him.

Maybe it's time that I start to believe him. I can jump because I know that he'll always catch me.

"We're meant to be, Iggy," he says quietly, and I sniffle, wiping away the tears.

"I know we are," I tell him.

"I love you."

I nod, clearing my throat as I look up to meet his green eyes.

"I love you too, Roman. I don't even know when it happened. It snuck up on me, but it's there and I don't want to get rid of this feeling."

"Good, 'cause I'm not going to let you."

His lips claim mine and I twine my arms around his neck, rising on my tiptoes to press my lips against his.

"Don't ever leave me again," he growls against my lips.

"I won't," I promise, pressing kisses against his face.

"Me and my wolf need you," he says, letting me pepper kisses all over him.

"I need you too."

"Then let's get out of here and go home."

I sink back to my feet, and Roman wraps his arm around my waist, not letting me get far.

"We'll go get your things and go home. We can leave your car with your parents and they can sell it if they need to. I'll get you something safer."

"You and my car," I grumble, and he smiles.

"I need to know that you're safe, and you can't be driving around the snowy roads in that thing."

I want to argue with him but I know it's a lost cause so I just nod.

"Fine. I can buy myself a car. I'll get a job in Aspen Ridge and save up."

"We have money," he says, and I shake my head.

"I still want to work."

"We'll talk about this later," he says as he starts to lead me to the front door.

"I have to tell Sharon that I'm quitting," I tell him, and he stops, waiting by the front door as I head over to my boss.

"I'm really sorry about this," I start, but Sharon just smiles.

"It's okay, dear. I always knew that you would leave someday. Be happy."

I smile, blinking away tears as I wrap Sharon up in a tight hug.

"Thank you for everything," I tell her sincerely, and she smiles as we pull apart.

"Enjoy your new man," she says, nodding to where Roman is impatiently waiting for me.

"I will," I say with a wide smile, and she laughs as I head over to my mate.

"Ready to go?" He asks, and I nod.

"Let's go."

There's still so much to do. We need to talk to my parents and get me moved out of their house, but I know that everything will be alright. As long as I have Roman at my side, then everything will work out just right.

He tucks me into his side, and I breathe in his familiar scent as I let him take me home.

TWELVE

Roman

FIVE YEARS LATER...

"YOU SHOULDN'T BE LIFTING THAT!" I snap when I walk into the house to see Iggy carrying a box downstairs.

My wolf is pacing inside me. He's always so anxious to see her when we get off work. It's been five years, and I know she won't leave us again, but we still can't relax until we see her face.

"It's light," she retorts, and I roll my eyes, storming over to my pregnant wife to take the box from her.

"How was work?" She asks, and I lean down, dropping a kiss on her lips before I follow her into the kitchen.

"Long. I missed you."

"Aww, I missed you too. You need to get dressed, though. Everyone will be here soon."

"For what?"

"The party," Iggy says easily, and I scan my brain, trying to remember if she mentioned it.

Iggy is at the forgetful stage of her pregnancy, and I don't think she told me we were having a party. I was looking forward to having some alone time with my wife, but she's obviously excited about this event so I suck it up and head upstairs to get dressed.

Iggy and I got married as soon as we got back to Aspen Ridge. I didn't want to wait another second to make her mine in every way. I added her to my bank account the day after, and she spent the first month turning our house into a home.

I love walking into a room now and seeing my mate's things everywhere. She's turned this sterile place into something warm and inviting. My wolf loves that her scent is all over this place.

I had hoped she would want to stay home, but I should have known better. Iggy couldn't seem to sit still for very long, and it was barely a month before she found herself a job and started working.

She's been helping Jax's mate, Parker, run the bakery in town for the last four and a half years. She's a terrible baker so she runs the front counter. I hate that she's away from me, but she loves getting out of the house and being social, and I love seeing her happy.

Now that we're close to expecting our first child, she's been cutting back on hours, and since Rue has kids now, too, she's been talking about becoming a stay-at-home mom, at least until our little one goes to school.

I walk past the nursery and sigh when I see that she hung the mobile above the crib at some point today. I'm always telling her to let me take care of things, but my Iggy is stubborn and too self-reliant.

"Mobile looks good," I call down to her as she walks past the bottom of the stairs.

"Thanks!"

She gives me a cheeky smile as she passes, and I roll my eyes, chuckling as I head into our bedroom to take a shower and get dressed.

My phone rings, and when I see that it's Jax, I answer.

"Did you know about this party?" He asks before I can get a word out.

"Nope, but apparently, it's happening. My mate is very excited about it."

"Same here. Do you need me to bring anything? Parker said we're having a bonfire and making s'mores."

"Dammit!" I shout, hurrying back downstairs.

"I'll get the smores sticks and start the fire," I shout to Iggy when I see her headed for the back door.

"Don't be silly. I can do it. You still need to get changed."

"Exactly, I'm all dirty, so let me go handle the firewood."

"Suit yourself," she says with a shrug, and I hurry outside.

"So? Bring anything?" Jax asks, making me realize that I'm still talking to him.

"How about a straight jacket for Iggy? I need her to stop trying to lift heavy things or strain herself too much."

"I'm not going back to the hospital, dude," he says, and I laugh.

"Fair enough. No, I think we're good."

"Cool. See you soon."

I end the call and head over to the wood pile to get the fire started. A Jeep pulls up out front, and I know without looking that it's Rue, Bo, and Liam.

"Hey! Need a hand?" Bo calls, and I nod.

"Sure."

Liam chases their little ones around the front yard, trying to steer them toward the front door, and Rue smiles, rubbing her pregnant stomach as she heads inside.

"Asa is getting bigger every time I see him," I comment, and Bo laughs.

"Rue says the same thing."

"How's the pregnancy going?" I ask.

"Good. She's a little worried about labor, but it will be alright."

I nod as we finish stacking the wood.

"I'll get this. Why don't you go help Iggy with that," he says, and I turn to see my mate trying to carry down some folding chairs.

"She just can't sit still," I groan, and my wolf sighs inside me as we jog over to help her.

"Take a break, mate," I order, and she rolls her eyes but nods.

She's winded, and I steer her over to where Rue is nibbling on some fruit.

"Why don't you two catch up?" I say before I head back outside.

She looks a little annoyed and I pull Iggy against me.

"What's wrong, mate?"

"My mom texted," she admits and I instantly understand her annoyance.

Iggy has her own debit and credit card. She's been added to my accounts since we got together and as soon as her parents realized that, they've been hitting her up like she's an ATM. We've been sending money to her parents every month to help out. I paid off quite a bit of their debt when we first married, but they always seem to find ways to take more on.

I think seeing that has helped Iggy realize that she isn't responsible for all of their money problems. I'm glad because I know she felt guilty that she couldn't do more to help them. Still, not she's starting to get tired of them only calling because they need something. I wish that I could protect her from them, but I can't. I suppose the next best thing is to surround her with people who truly love her.

More cars pull up, and I smile as I finish setting up the chairs and head upstairs to change. Voices fill the house, and my wolf curls up inside me, happy to be surrounded by our family and friends.

Life used to be boring and monotonous. I went to work and I went home. The days were starting to run together in one giant blur, and then I met Iggy.

She's flipped my whole world upside down. She drives me crazy, makes me laugh, and puts me at ease all at once. She's the best thing that ever happened to me, and even though it seems weird, I'm so glad she was swept up in that avalanche and into my life.

I don't know what I would do without her, and luckily for my wolf and me, we'll never have to find out.

Ingram Content Group UK Ltd.
Milton Keynes UK
UKHW011532040723
424531UK00001B/40